Emma Lea's Magic Teapot

Written by Babette Donaldson • Illustrated by Jerianne Van Dijk

Published by Blue Gate Books, Nevada City, California

Requests for permission to make copies of any part of the work should be mailed to:
Permissions Department
Blue Gate Books
P.O. Box 2137
Nevada City, CA 95959
(530) 478-0365

Summary: Emma Lea dreams that her new teapot is magic,
granting her three special wishes.

ISBN: 978-0-9792612-1-3

[1. Juvenile Fiction 2. Tea 3. Family & Friends 4. Magic]

Library of Congress Control Number: 2007905404

Printed in China

Blue Gate Books
P.O. Box 2137
Nevada City, CA 95959

Design and computer production by Patty Arnold
Menagerie Design and Publishing
www.menageriedesign.net

It is often said by tea lovers that we see the world in our teacups.
We taste the environment where the tea plant grew
and we savor the season when the leaves were plucked.
In countries where our tea grows, it is a way of life.
And it is an art.

I dedicate this book to the plantation workers
who infuse a bit of magic into my favorite daily brews.

When Emma Lea finished her tea
with Theodosia Teddy Bear,
Daddy came in to read
a bedtime story.

"This is my favorite."
He found the page in the thick
storybook. "Aladdin's Magic Lamp."

It was the story of a young boy
receiving three wishes from the
genie in a magic lamp.

Daddy enjoyed it
so much, he kept
reading even after
Emma Lea's eyes
became tired
and heavy
and the
words
melted
into a
dream.

The genie of the story
changed into her
grandmother.
Grammy floated
out of her
teapot in
a puff of
smoke.

She told Emma Lea
to rub the teapot
and make three wishes.

It was a wonderful dream.
Emma Lea woke up wanting
to believe it was real.

The room was as bright as
morning. The full moon
spotlighted Emma Lea's
teapot on the table.
It looked like it was
glowing with a
light of its own.

She jumped out of bed and put both hands on the sides of her glowing teapot. She rubbed until the warmth of her hands also warmed the china.

"First," I wish Mama would make my favorite breakfast."
Emma Lea was hungry just thinking about the way Mama
rolled chunks of banana and strawberry into thin pancakes
and drizzled them with raspberry syrup. She hadn't fixed them
since Emma Lea's birthday breakfast. That seemed much too long ago.

"Second," she chose the wish carefully, "I want Sam to be my best
friend again." She was still sad about what had happened at school.
Sam's feelings were hurt by something she said. She had left
school feeling like it was the worst day of her life.

She rubbed so hard, she turned the pot
sideways and spilled the leftover tea
from Theodosia's cup.

"Third, I want to sing
in the school talent show."
She had been too scared
to go to the auditions with Sam.
"I told him it was a stupid song,"
she explained to Theodosia.
"The truth is, I was afraid."

Emma Lea took Theodosia back to bed with her.
"The argument with Sam was my fault. I hope my teapot wish
will fix things between us."

The cuddly bear helped her go back to sleep.

The next thing she knew, the light coming through her window
was morning sun. She wondered if the wishes had been real.
But then, she saw the tea stain
on the tablecloth.

That proved it had been
more than just a dream.
And the smell of
breakfast told her
that her first wish
was already
coming true.

Emma Lea ran to the kitchen and helped Mama roll the fruit inside the pancakes. "Tunnels of Love, is what the recipe is called," Mama told her.

It was difficult to keep her secret about the teapot and the wishes. But, with only one wish-come-true it was too soon to tell.

Emma Lea carefully drizzled the syrup on Daddy's Tunnels of Love.

Mama poured the breakfast tea and Daddy said it would be OK to be a little bit late for work on this special morning. He waited to drive Emma Lea to school.

"Daddy," she wanted to tell him but she was a little worried that it might spoil the magic.

"Yes, Emmie?"

"This feels like a very magical day."
It was like telling only half of her secret.

"It does, indeed." Daddy said and kissed her on her forehead before she scooted out the door of the car.

Sam was waiting at their special spot on the playground, watching through the diamond-shaped holes in the wire fence. She waved and ran to meet him.

"I'm sorry." She wanted to say a lot more but he interrupted.

"That's OK." he said. "It's a silly old talent show, anyhow. I just like singing with you. I don't care if anyone else hears us."

Her second wish was coming true.

Emma Lea and Sam climbed to the top of the monkey bars and sang their song. They were best friends again.

Mr. Ondi, the teacher in charge of the talent show, heard them. "We need a song just like yours to start the show. Will you do it?"

They answered by singing the last chorus louder and better than ever. This was Emma Lea's third wish come true.

Now, she wanted to tell everyone. But she only told Sam.

"You didn't need to use one of your wishes on me. We will always be best friends," he told her.

When Mama picked her up from school,
she sang out the news.

"The teapot Grammy gave me is magic! I made three wishes. They all came true.
It's magic. It's really, really magic." She explained about the first wish
for the special breakfast and the second wish about Sam and
the last wish about the talent show.

When Daddy got home,
Emma Lea asked him to
read the story again. She wanted to
get three more wishes.
She wanted a puppy and a new bike and . . .
"I wish Grammy and Grampop
were here right now!"

addy listened patiently and carefully before he said, "I don't think the magic is in the teapot."

He took both of her hands and held them in his own. "Mama and I are celebrating the anniversary of the day we got married. The strawberry-banana pancakes are our favorites too. We had them for breakfast on our honeymoon. That's why we still call them Tunnels of Love."

"My teapot isn't really magic," she said, sadly.

Daddy tried to copy her sad face but ended up looking
silly and making her laugh. Emma Lea knew
he was trying to cheer her up.

"You don't have to make wishes for special family time,"
Daddy agreed. He let Emma Lea climb into his lap.

"That's what Sam said about my second wish."

"Friendship is a very powerful magic."
Daddy's hug made her feel much better.
She started to think about her wishes
in a different way.

"Maybe my wish about the talent show came true
because I'm so happy when I sing."

Daddy nodded. "There is a very big magic when you
find the talents that give you joy. We all love to
hear you sing."

He kissed her on her blushing cheek.
But he didn't kiss away her sad thought.

"There wasn't anything special about my wishes."

"I'm not so sure," Mama said as she came in
with Emma Lea's teapot on a tray with their
teacups and treats. She pointed at the little
window beside the front door. They could see
Grammy and Grampop ready to ring the bell.

"That's four." Her sadness was gone.
Emma Lea danced with delight.

"What's this?" Grammy and Grampop both asked when they saw Emma Lea's delight.

"Magic," she managed to whisper the first time. "Teapot magic," she said louder the second time. "You're my fourth wish-come-true." And she sputtered out the whole story.

She was so excited she didn't notice the large box Grampop had brought inside. When she told Grammy about her wish for a puppy, she stopped to take a deep breath and she heard soft whimpering.

"I've come to believe," Grampop said as he opened the top of the box, "that this is a very magical world indeed."

When Emma Lea looked at Grammy, she remembered the dream. Grammy's smile was the same. The warm, happy feeling was the same.

"Not just my teapot?" Emma Lea asked.

Wishes · Magic · Dreams · Friendship

"Much more than that," Daddy said as he pulled the squirmy puppy out of the box.

"I've been calling her Oolong," Grammy said. "She's the soft, golden color of my favorite kind of tea." – Grampop made a face. "Who ever heard of a dog named Oolong."

"We could call her Ginger." Emma Lea asked as the puppy chased her around the room and out the front. "I love it when you put a little piece of sweet ginger in my tea."

"Ginger is an excellent name," Grampop agreed.

Emma Lea stopped and looked around the yard as Daddy snapped the leash onto Ginger's collar.

"What is it?" Mama asked.

"Oh, just wondering
   about the bike," Emma Lea answered
with a big smile. "But I think I'd rather
save some of my wishes for another day.

Tunnels of Love Makes 8 "Tunnels"

Crepe Batter

Sift together: 1 cup flour   1 teaspoon baking powder

                  1 pinch salt   2 tablespoons powdered sugar

Beat separately: 1 egg

Add to beaten egg:

                  1 cup milk   1/2 teaspoon vanilla or lemon juice

Blend milk and egg into flour mixture and let set 30 minutes or overnight.

To cook crepes:

Heat small skillet and add a few drops of vegetable oil to the pan for each crepe. Add a small quantity of the thin batter and shake or tip the pan to have it flow over the surface of the pan.

Cook each crepe quickly over moderate heat. Allow it to lightly brown on one side. Lift it gently with a fork or spatula and flip to cook the other side.

Crepes can be cooked prior to filling and set aside. If they are not overcooked, they will remain soft and can be rolled with the filling.

Filling:

                  3 - 4 bananas

                  16 — 20 strawberries

                  Raspberry Sauce

Cut bananas into 1/2 inch rounds. Cut strawberries into small pieces. On top of each open crepe, create a row of banana rounds with space for the chopped strawberries. Drizzle raspberry sauce over the fruit filling and roll into a tunnel. Drizzle more raspberry sauce over the top and serve immediately.

Options:

• Use fresh raspberries and crush into a juicy sauce, cooking over low heat with a bit of honey or sugar, sweetening to your taste.

• Top with sour cream, Devonshire Cream or Lemon Curd or sprinkle with powdered sugar.

Raspberries, blueberries or blackberries can be substituted for strawberries or mixed together for a special berry treat.

AUTHOR

BABETTE DONALDSON is the author and creator of the Emma Lea stories. She has a BA in Creative Writing and a BFA in Ceramic Art from San Francisco State University and received her tea certification from the Specialty Tea Institute, the education division of The Tea Council of the United States. She is currently the director of Tea Suite, a non-profit organization supporting art education.

ILLUSTRATOR

JERIANNE VAN DIJK — An artist for over 30 years, Jerianne Van Dijk's award-winning illustrations have graced calendars, greeting cards, product labels, posters and books. She is proficient in various media and is as happy doing botanicals as goofy whimsical things to make you think. Jerianne began working as a graphic designer for an array of advertising agencies, newspapers, and printing companies. She particularly enjoys freelance illustration as one of her many specialties. Residing in Northern California as a watercolor instructor, fine artist and illustrator Jerianne enjoys the work her gift affords her. For more about her work visit www.jerianne.net

DESIGNER

PATTY ARNOLD is the owner of *Menagerie Design and Publishing*–a small company specializing in book production. She has a BFA in sculpture and printmaking, a BS in Graphic Communications and an MFA in Photography and Digital Imaging. She also teaches Graphic Design, Typography and Digital Arts at the local community college and is an exhibiting photographer. You can view her fine art at www.pattyarnold.com and her design projects at www.menageriedesign.net.

More Magic Teapot Stories Online:

The magic brewing in Emma Lea's new teapot doesn't end with this book. Join her for a new story, *Teapot Magic for Sam*, on our website www.emmaleabooks.com. This online story is available without charge.

OTHER EMMA LEA BOOKS:

Emma Lea's First Tea Party

Emma Lea is excited to attend the annual tea party with the ladies of the family. They celebrate Grammy's birthday with a special dress up event. "I want to look like a big girl for Grammy," she tells her mother.

The table is elegantly set with Grammy's finest china and trays of teacakes when Emma Lea and her mother arrive. But Emma Lea brings some new twists to the old family tradition.

ISBN: 978-0-9792612-0-6 • $16.95

Available at teashops and bookstores. To find locations near you, visit our website,

www.emmaleabooks.com

COMING SOON

Emma Lea's First Tea Ceremony
Available, December 2007

Tea With Daddy
Available, March 2008

During these chaotic days of unrest around the world, we often feel helpless and alone. Sip for Peace reminds us that tea connects the world. It has inspired great thinkers of the past and has the potential to fuel powerful visions for a better future. The Tea Sippers Society invites you to share this practice during January 2018.

What is "Sip for Peace"?

Sip for Peace is a personal practice using the mindfulness of making a simple cup of tea to inspire a vision of living in a peaceful world. During the month of January 2018, Tea Sippers will also share a virtual celebration using the following resources:

Daily emails pairing a meditation on World Peace with a tea culture.

- ~ **Meditations** by noted Tea Writers & Philosophers
- ~ Explorations of 31 **Tea Growing Regions**

A Global Tea Blend - a limited edition blend from these 31 regions.

"Sip In" events with family, friends or a community group; Schools, Libraries, Tearooms or other kinds of Meet-ups.

Celebration beings January 1, 2018 - Become a Tea Sipper Now

Forever Free Tea Sipper Membership Includes:

- All-Access To *Sip For Peace* Event
- Access to 50%+ of the ITSS Internet Content
- Download tea activity book *Fun-With-Tea* ($16.00 value)
- Monthly Newsletter Updates & Member Specials
- Tea Event Calendar & Tea Business Directory
- Plus new content added regularly

International
Tea Sippers
Society

Full Sipper Memberships ($25) Include:

- Forever Free content + 100% of ITSS website content
- Complete Emma Lea E-Book Series - Download PDFs
- Online viewing and downloads of out-of-print Tea Classics
- Special offers and opportunities.

TeaSippersSociety.com

When the Kettle Whistles

To the tune of "White Coral Bells"

Lyrics by Babette Donaldson

a Traditional English round

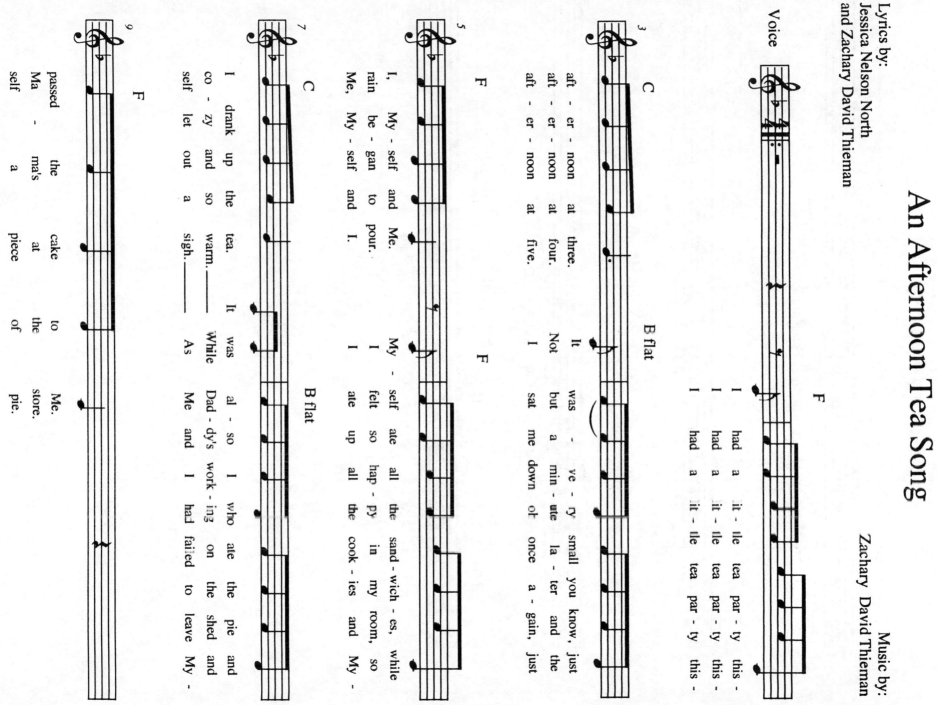

An Afternoon Tea Song

Lyrics by:
Jessica Nelson North
and Zachary David Thieman

Music by:
Zachary David Thieman

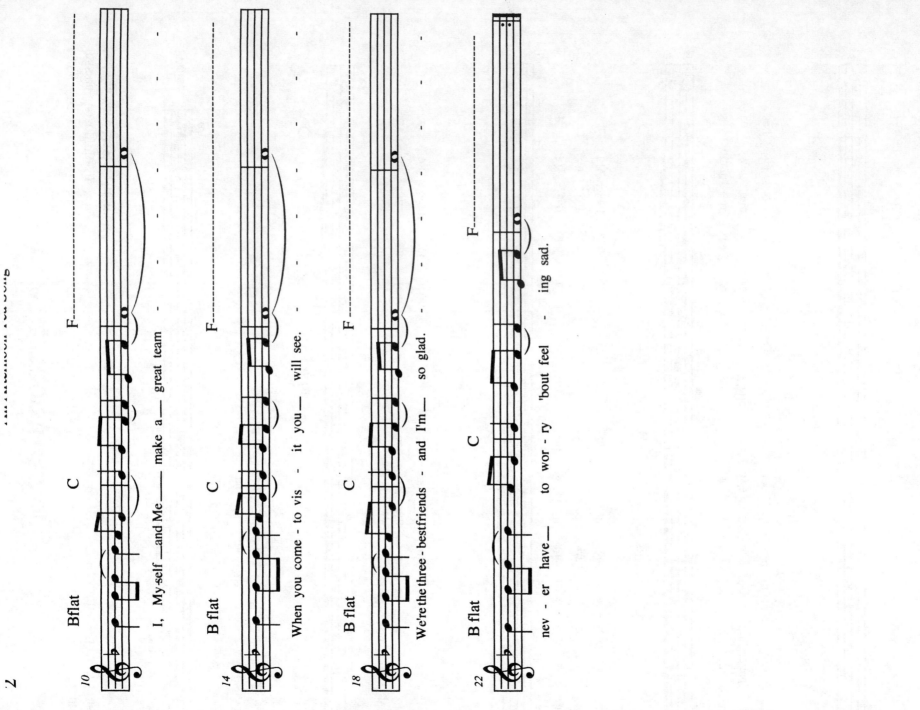

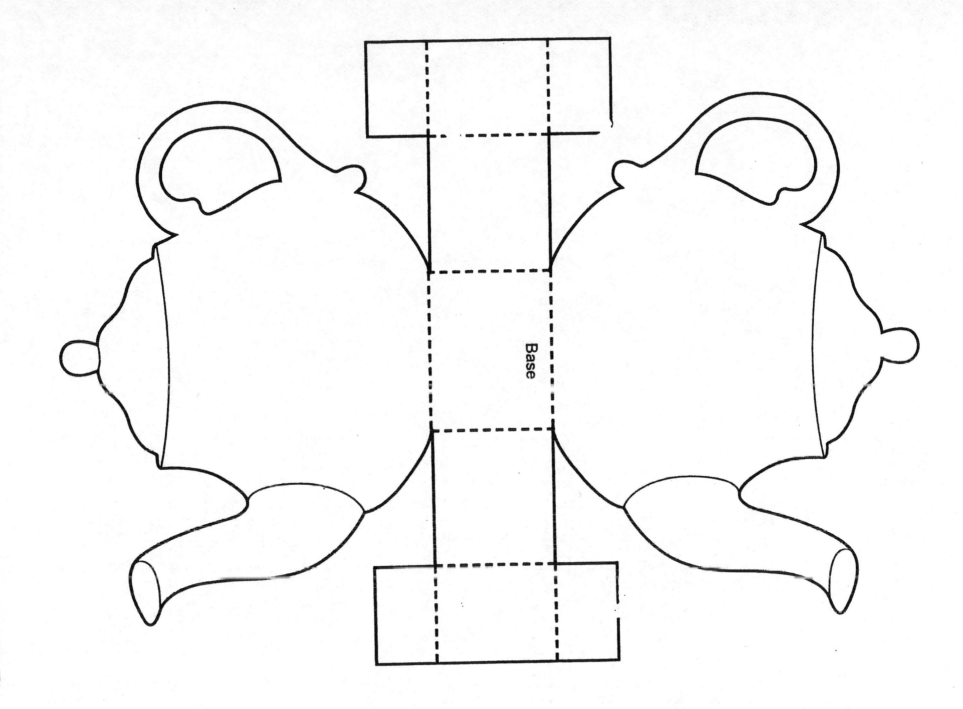

Base

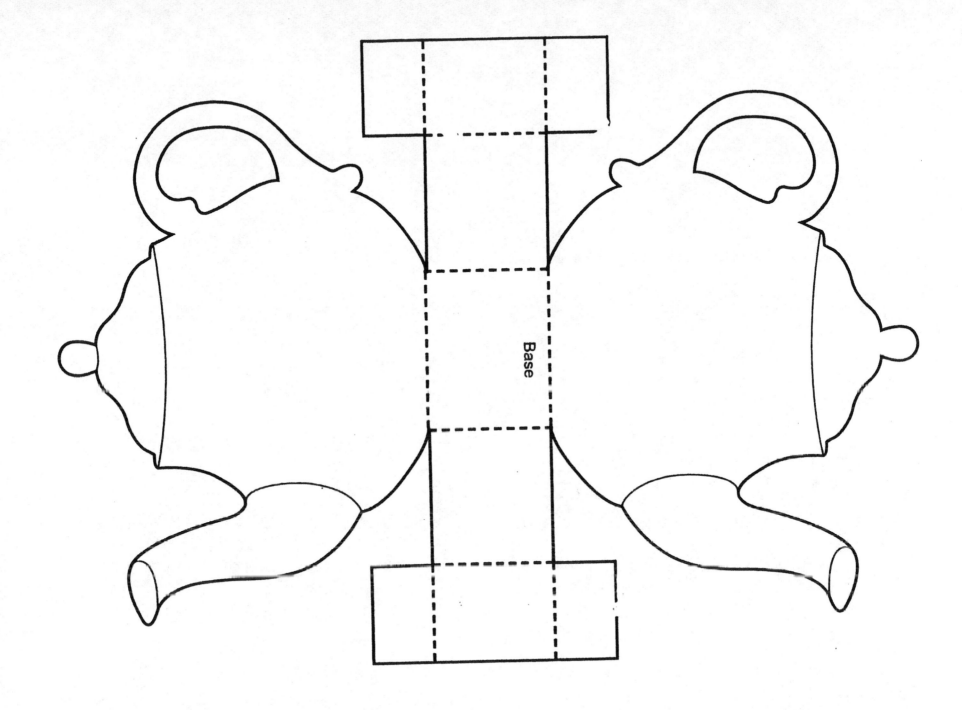

Base